© World rights
Sandviks Bokforlag a.s.
Stavanger, Norway

Published in 1992 by
Tormont Publications Inc.
338 Saint Antoine St. East
Montreal, Canada H2Y 1A3
Tel. (514) 954-1441   Fax (514) 954-1443

ISBN 2-89429-141-8

Printed in Belgium

THE
TROLL CHILDREN
AND THE
PRINCESS

Story by:
Eli Aleksandersen Cantillon

Illustrations:
François Ruyer

Design:
Lene Eintveit

"Hush," Aja said suddenly. "Stay quiet!" and she signalled to Uffe, Olle and little Klaffe, who were playing noisily in the field next to the forest. Her brothers stopped their game and stood as quiet as statues, listening.

"I don't hear anything," little Klaffe soon said, and started to kick the ball again. But Aja held her finger to her lips and gave him a cross look which made him stop at once. Aja could be a very strict little troll when she was in the mood for it.

In the silence, Aja heard the sound again. "There. Did you hear that?" she whispered. "I think someone is crying."

The others nodded, their eyes wide. They heard it too.

The four troll children crept towards the sound, which seemed to be coming from the forest. They tiptoed between the bushes and around the great trees as quietly as they could.

3

The sobbing was louder now, and they could catch glimpses of something white in the dark woods. As they tiptoed closer, they realized it was a girl with long fair hair and a long white dress. She was sitting on a rock, and sobbing so hard that her whole body trembled.

"Poor little thing," Aja said, which made her brothers giggle, because the girl was so much bigger than Aja.

Aja grabbed Olle and Klaffe by the hand and motioned to Uffe to follow her. Then she marched straight up to the girl.

"Ah hmmm..." Aja said. But the girl did not hear her because she was crying so hard.

"Can we help you?" Aja tried again. This time the girl peered through her fingers at the four little trolls. At once, she stopped crying, let out a yell, jumped down from the rock and scooted behind the nearest tree. The troll children looked at each other in astonishment. Was it possible the girl with the long fair hair was afraid of them?

Aja spied something glittering in the grass beside the rock. She stooped to pick it up, and realized with amazement that it was a small golden crown.

"Is this yours?" she asked, holding it out. The fair-haired girl nodded, wiping the tears from her cheeks.

"Who are you?" Uffe asked.

"Why are you crying?" piped up Olle.

"Are you sad?" asked little Klaffe, and toddled up to her. He took hold of her hand and stroked it gently.

Realizing the troll children were harmless, the girl shyly came out from behind the tree.

"I am Princess Lara," she said, "and that is my crown."

She took the crown from Aja, and placed it on top of her long fair hair.

"I was crying because I have lost my horse. We were out riding in the forest. We stopped beside a big lake to rest, and I fell asleep. When I woke up, Lilja was gone," the Princess told them.

"Lilja. What a pretty name!" said little Klaffe.

"I called her Lilja because she is as white as a lily," the Princess explained. "I've been looking for her for hours, and I think I'm lost. I've never been this far from the castle before!" she said, looking as if she were going to cry again. "Don't worry. We'll help you find her," Aja said. Her brothers all nodded in agreement. "Let's start right away!" Uffe said. And off they all went.

The Princess and the troll children walked a long time until they came to a small lake. They stopped to rest, and Uffe and Olle dipped their toes in the water. It was a hot day, and the sun shining through the treetops made beautiful patterns on the ground.

Suddenly Aja heard a soft rustling sound.
She noticed movement in the tall grass, as if the wind
were blowing it. But there was no wind! Before Aja knew
what to think, out popped five little heads topped
with five little red hats.

"Oats!" one of the little heads said loudly, startling
the Princess and the troll children.

"What kinds of creatures are you?" exclaimed Princess Lara.

"No time to talk," the little fellow said. "Have you seen our oats?"

"Oats?" repeated Aja in surprise. "What oats?"

"The sack of oats that I've been collecting all day with the other gnomes," he said. "We need them to make porridge. But we stopped for a swim at the big lake in the forest, and when we came out of the water, our sack had disappeared. We have to find it, or we'll starve this winter," the gnome said.

"That's right," grumbled the other gnomes.

"We haven't seen any sack," the Princess said. "We were looking for my horse, Lilja. But maybe we can help you look for your sack, too. We certainly don't want you to starve," she added.

Aja and her brothers agreed. And so they all set off together, the Princess, the four troll children, and the five little gnomes.

One of the gnomes, the one called Gnomeri, made up
a little song, and they all sang it as they marched along.
(Tune: Oh Tannenbaum)

> A gnome must eat, a gnome must eat,
> A gnome must have his porridge sweet.
> And if he has no porridge sweet,
> He must eat bark, and that's no treat.
> A gnome must eat, a gnome must eat
> To keep his strength in arms and feet.

"This is no time for songs and nonsense!" grumbled the oldest gnome.
But the others just laughed.

"There can't be any harm in having some fun while we search," said Gnomeri, and he made up another verse.

We met a lovely princess here,
Who has just brushed away a tear.
Her horse has been away a while
And we have searched and walked a mile.
Our feet are sore, our eyes they sting,
And now we're not allowed to sing.

Hearing this, even the oldest gnome had to chuckle, and he started to sing along with the others.

After a while, they arrived on the grassy shores of a large lake.

"This is where Lilja and I stopped to rest," the Princess told her new friends.

"How strange," the oldest gnome said. "This is the very place we left our sack of oats while we went for a swim!"

The troll brothers were thinking hard. "Someone must have stolen them both," Uffe said.

"It must be a thief!" Olle said.

Princess Lara was shocked. "I can't believe anyone would steal Lilja while I slept," she said. "No one could be that wicked!"

"And who would dare steal our oats from under our noses?" Gnomeri added angrily.

"It must be a very wicked thief," little Klaffe said.

Aja was a very sensible little troll. "Let's split up into two groups and search all around the lake," she suggested. "If there were thieves, they might have left some tracks. If we search the ground carefully, we might find out which way they went."

Uffe and Olle went in one direction with three of the gnomes. Princess Lara, Aja and little Klaffe set off in the other direction with Gnomeri and the oldest gnome.

The old gnome immediately decided he should be the leader. "It's only natural," he said. He made them line up side by side, and told them to search every bit of ground for clues.

But little Klaffe soon decided it was all very boring.

"I'd rather go up on that hill and look for berries," he told his sister.

"All right," Aja told him. "But don't wander off."

Little Klaffe soon found a little patch of ripe berries, and sat down to eat. From the hill, he could see his sister and brothers searching the shores. When he had eaten every berry, he looked around for another patch.

Suddenly, he spied something shining in the grass a little farther up the hill. Curious, he picked it up. It was a silvery colored curved object, with holes in it. It looked almost like a circle that had been broken in half.

Klaffe had no idea what it was, so he put it in his pocket. Then he went back down the hill to join his sister and the Princess.

As night approached, Uffe, Olle and the three gnomes returned from the other direction. No one had found any trace of the thieves. It was a very disappointed group that sat by the lake that night in the sunset.

The gnomes gathered some dry wood, and the oldest gnome lit them a fire. "At least we can keep warm for the night," he said.

They sat talking around the fire for a long time, trying to figure out what could have happened to Lilja and the sack of oats. To cheer them up, Gnomeri sang some old gnome songs.

They were so amusing that even the Princess had to laugh.

After a while, little Klaffe could barely keep his eyes open. "I think I want to go to sleep," he said, and snuggled up against the Princess.

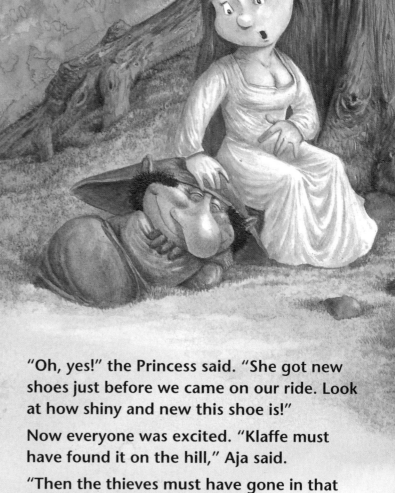

But he couldn't get comfortable with the mysterious object in his pocket, so he took it out, and set in on the ground.

Princess Lara took one look at the silvery object and became very excited.

"Why, that's Lilja's shoe!" she exclaimed.

"Are you sure?" the oldest gnome asked.

"Oh, yes!" the Princess said. "She got new shoes just before we came on our ride. Look at how shiny and new this shoe is!"

Now everyone was excited. "Klaffe must have found it on the hill," Aja said.

"Then the thieves must have gone in that direction, because Lilja and I never went on the hill," Princess Lara said.

"Help! Ghosts! The ghosts are after me," the creature yelled. As it came closer, they realized it was a very frightened looking fox.

"Ghosts. Terrible. Don't go up there," he stuttered, panting to catch his breath after his wild race down the hill.

"Now, now," said the oldest gnome. "Take a deep breath, and tell us everything from the beginning."

"I was out hunting all night," the fox began. "I had no luck, so at dawn I decided to rest in an old barn I know about. But when I got there, I heard strange sounds inside. I didn't dare go in, but I peeped through the window, and that's when I saw them!" the fox gasped.

By now, everyone was feeling much cheerier. At least they knew which direction to search. "But we'll have to wait until the sun comes up," the oldest gnome said wisely.

They were so excited, it took them a long time to fall asleep. But finally they all dozed off.

Daylight was just breaking when they were wakened by loud shouts. Rubbing the sleep from their eyes, they saw something far up the hill, scrambling towards them.

"Ghosts!" he said,
pointing wildly up the hill.

"How do you know they were
ghosts?" Aja asked. "Could you
see them clearly?"

"Well, maybe not that clearly,"
the fox admitted. "But I definitely
saw something white moving
around in there!"

Princess Lara, the troll children and the five gnomes exchanged glances. They were all thinking the same thing.

"We don't think it was ghosts you saw," Aja said. "But it might have been some very wicked thieves."

"Thieves!" the fox shrieked. "Why, they're even more dangerous than ghosts!" And with that, he dashed off into the forest.

"What a cowardly fox," the oldest gnome said, shaking his head.

The others laughed, but they were actually quite scared themselves. The important thing, though, was to get Lilja and the sack of oats back. So after a quick breakfast, they headed up the hill.

When they arrived at the top, they could see the old barn the fox had described. It was down in a valley, next to a huge old oak tree. Nervously, they headed down the hill, careful not to step on any dry twigs. They didn't want the thieves to hear them coming!

When they reached the barn, they all hid behind the big oak tree. Whispering, they tried to decide what to do next. Somebody had to frighten away the thieves, while the rest of them saved Lilja and the sack of oats. "I should be the one, because it's my horse they stole," Princess Lara said bravely.

She marched up to the barn door, and shouted as loud as she could: "The King's daughter orders all the thieves hiding in the barn to come out right now!" Nothing happened.

She hollered again. "Come out right now. Or I will make sure you will have to peel potatoes in the King's palace for the rest of your lives. And that is a big job. You have no idea how many guests we have for dinner every night!"

The troll children giggled, knowing that Princess Lara was far too kind to let anyone be punished *that* severely.

Suddenly, the barn door squeaked slowly open. Everyone held their breath in excitement and fear. Then, a shaggy white head appeared. As it crept shyly out of the barn, they realized it was a brand new baby foal, still a little wobbly on its legs. And right behind the foal was the most beautiful white horse the troll children had ever seen.

"Lilja!" the Princess shrieked. And she threw her arms around the horse's strong neck. "Lilja, you're safe! I was so worried!"

Meanwhile, the oldest gnome had crept into the barn, and carefully examined every corner. When he came back out, he was smiling and carrying a big sack. "Well, there are no thieves in there," he said. "But we've solved the mystery of the missing sack!"

"What do you mean?" Aja asked.

The old gnome explained that Lilja had taken the oats. "She realized she would need some food while she hid away to give birth to the little foal," he said.

"Is this really Lilja's foal?" the Princess asked. But of course, everyone could see that the foal looked just like his mother, and they all did a happy little dance.

Then the Princess noticed Gnomeri looking into the sack. It seemed that Lilja had eaten quite a bit of of the oats. "Don't worry," she said. "My father will give you *two* sacks of oats for helping find Lilja!"

The gnomes were overjoyed. Now they would have enough oats to last them all winter and the next winter as well.

"Now that we don't have to worry about having enough food, I want everyone to come back to our place for a porridge party," the oldest gnome said. And they all set off, singing a happy gnome song.

The porridge party was a great success, with gnomes of all ages and sizes bringing them as much sweet porridge as they could eat. Then a gnome band played and everyone danced and sang for the rest of the afternoon.

As evening approached, Aja realized that she and her brothers should set off for home. "Mother will be worried," she told them.

Princess Lara was anxious to go home too, and offered the troll children a ride. "Don't worry, you're so small that Lilja can easily carry us all," she said. So they all climbed on, and the little foal trotted along beside them.

The troll children were so tired from all the excitement that they barely talked all the way home.

When they arrived at the field next to the trolls' cave, Princess Lara helped the troll children off the horse. "I've been thinking," she said. "I really appreciate how you helped me find Lilja, and I would like to give you a present. As soon as Lilja's foal is big enough to leave his mother, I want you to have him. But you have to promise that we can meet often, so the foal can visit his mother."

Aja, Uffe and Olle were so pleased and surprised that they barely knew what to say. They just jumped up and down with excitement and gave the Princess lots of warm hugs.

Only little Klaffe was silent. He had already fallen asleep, his funny little hat pulled down over his ears and a big smile on his face.